In a certain time, in a certain land,
once there lived and once there was...

 Published by Grosset & Dunlap, a member of The Putnam Publishing Group, New York. Published simultaneously in Canada. Printed in the United States of America. Book design by Lynn Braswell.
Library of Congress Catalog Card Number 85-12709 ISBN: 0-448-10281-1 A B C D E F G H I J

Santa Claus

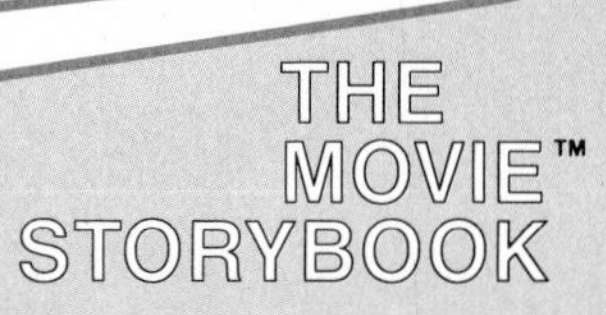

By JOAN D. VINGE

BASED ON A STORY BY
DAVID & LESLIE NEWMAN,

SCREENPLAY BY
DAVID NEWMAN

GROSSET & DUNLAP,
NEW YORK

The icy wind swept over the dark pine forests, bearing on its back yet another blizzard to be dumped on the rudely built dwellings huddled among the trees below.

This was a Christmas Eve long, long ago when all the people of the village put aside the problems of their daily existence for a brief time. It also promised a time of quiet celebration . . . and a very special visitor. Already the older children were beginning to grow restless, waiting for him, although the younger ones still sat in a circle listening raptly to one of Grandmother's stories.

". . . suddenly the ice mountains cracked open, and beautiful, beautiful lights shone in the sky." The old woman spread her arms, smiling. "And out came the *vendegum.* Those are the little men who live in the ice mountains way up at the top of the world, under the North Star."

"This is the same story she told last year," Hans murmured to himself, over by the window. He was thirteen, and had decided that he knew too much to listen to children's fairy tales.

Stubbornly he peeped out through the thick glass panes again, squinting into the storm. He grinned, as all at once a sleigh took form in the shapeless whiteness of the farmyard. "It's them!" he shouted triumphantly. "Here they come!"

The open sleigh, drawn by two reindeer, pulled up before the barn door. A stocky man in his late fifties climbed down from its seat and offered his hand to its other occupant.

His wife, Anya, pushed aside her lap robe and climbed down to stand in the snow beside him. She smiled as she saw the anticipation in his eyes.

As they entered the barn, the waiting children swarmed around them, laughing and shouting. The clamoring children were hugging Claus and pulling at the bulging sack he carried. In a grinning chorus they cried, "Happy Christmas, Uncle Claus!"

Beaming with pleasure and pride, Claus began to take from the bag, one at a time, a wonderful assortment of hand-carved wooden toys.

Anya watched her husband with the children, her eyes shining.

"How lucky you are, Anya," Marta said softly.

Lucky? she thought. *To be married for thirty years to a wonderful man who loves children so, and never blessed with one of our own?*

The evening passed swiftly for the happy adults and children, with much laughter and little thought of the worsening weather outside. Only Claus's reindeer, tethered to a fence post in the yard, were aware of the rising wind, the deepening snow.

Axel, Hans's father, went to the window, rubbing away the frost to peer outside. "Claus, stay the night," he urged. "You can't get through."

"With my reindeer?" Claus laughed, trying to reassure him. "Donner and Blitzen can get through anything!"

The couple left the barn, carrying the warm wishes of the others with them into the stormy night.

Donner and Blitzen snorted and shuddered as Claus tugged on the reins. With a final wave to the friends still gathered in the doorway, he started the sleigh on its way down the nearly invisible road.

The wind-blown snow was sweeping out of the blackness directly into their faces now. Claus slapped the reins. "Come on, Blitzen, pull harder!" he shouted sharply.

After a while Anya looked at him with frightened eyes. "Are we lost?" she asked.

"I can't see the road," Claus's own fears took on the terrifying reality of words, as he suddenly realized that the sleigh had stopped moving.

"Blast!" Claus climbed down. As he reached the pair of familiar, velvet-antlered heads, he stopped short, feeling a chill far sharper than the freezing air. The team of reindeer stood motionless, their dark eyes glazed with a strange torpor. As he watched, Blitzen suddenly slumped in his traces and fell to his knees.

"Get up!" he blustered, trying now to bully the torpid animal into action. "You want to stay here and freeze to death?"

Suddenly Donner slumped to his knees beside Blitzen. Claus backed away, his concern deepening into real fear.

"Claus!" Anya's voice cried, rising with her own fear, *"Come back! I can't see you!"*

Claus ran back to the sleigh and climbed up into the seat beside her. But even as she lifted her head to meet his gaze, her eyes dimmed and flickered shut, and she sagged against him, unconscious.

"Oh my God! Anya—" Claus gasped. But the same creeping lethargy began to lay its icy fingers on him, stealing away his strength. This couldn't be happening to him, not on Christmas, when he had not yet delivered his last toy....

The relentless wind and snow closed in about them, covering them with a blanket of white, until they were utterly lost in the storm.

Donner woke with a snort and struggled to his feet. The storm, the wind, the driving snow had all disappeared—and with them, the forest. He stood on a frozen plain that was completely devoid of trees, beneath a sky glittering with stars of incredible brightness.

Then Donner snorted loudly, trying to get the attention of his master and mistress. Claus started awake at the sound.

"Anya," he whispered. Anya's eyes widened like his own.

The North Star hung directly overhead, and far brighter than it had ever looked before. The finger of its light seemed to point downward toward the snow-covered plain ahead of them... where now a glorious array of twinkling lights filled the space between heaven and earth.

"What?" Anya whispered tremulously.

As the streaming lights came closer, they began to see that each light was a separate candle, each held aloft by a small being that looked very much like a miniature human.

One of the creatures stepped forward. He was an elderly man, with sparse white hair and a ruddy wrinkled face, framed by long mutton-chop whiskers.

"Welcome!" the white-haired elf cried.

"The . . . the . . . *vendegum?"* Claus gasped, barely able to speak.

"We prefer to be called elves, if you don't mind," he said pleasantly.

"You . . . you . . . you . . .," Claus began, but couldn't finish his sentence.

"I'm called Dooley," the spokesman continued, smiling. "We've been expecting you for a long, long time. We almost gave up hope."

Claus shook his head. "Where are we?" he whispered.

"Home," Dooley said, and gestured toward the lights.

"No, no, no," Anya protested, lifting her hand to point. "Our home is far from—"

"Not anymore," Dooley interrupted gently. "This is your home now."

Behind them, as they spoke, four elves slipped away from the larger gathering and moved quietly around behind the sleigh.

The leader of the foray was an impulsive young elf called Patch—because, as the bright green patch on the knee of his pants suggested, he had more important things to think about than the state of his clothes. His quick, creative mind was as bright as a star, but as undisciplined as it was unique.

"Hi, there!" Patch said to Claus, who stared at him with complete incredulity.

"Welcome aboard, sir. Speaking for the boys and myself—" He waved his hands like an amateur magician. "You must be the missus!" he almost shouted.

"Me?" Anya said dazedly.

"We knew you'd be nice, but we didn't expect someone so pretty and young."

"Oh my . . .," Anya said, and blushed becomingly. She had not heard such a compliment in some time.

Dooley pushed forward. "My friends, let us show you your new home," he said to Claus and Anya, guiding them back into their sleigh.

"I don't understand," Claus murmured. "You said our new home? But there's nothing here."

"Look again," Dooley said, smiling.

Claus and Anya looked out again at the empty wastes of snow. And as they watched, an entire village suddenly shimmered into existence.

A broad pathway marked by fir trees and warmly glowing lanterns led across the snow to the distant village. The village itself was for very small people. Claus and Anya could see countless tiny separate eaves and turrets and chimneys protruding everywhere, all thickly frosted with snow like an enchanted gingerbread house.

"Come, fellow elves!" Dooley called out to the gathered elves. "Take them to their home!"

Claus and Anya, perched high on its seat, clung to the sleigh and each other, wide-eyed, as the elves began to draw it toward their village.

When they had reached the village gates at last, Claus and Anya climbed down from the sleigh while an elf named Boog led the reindeer along behind them.

Patch stepped forward, seizing Claus and Anya each by an arm, and drawing them aside toward the waiting entrance. "Right this way, folks," barked Patch. "Sixty rooms, hot and cold running ice cubes and a southern exposure in every direction. This *is* the North Pole, after all."

Claus and Anya had stepped through the doorway into another world. A panorama of dazzling, dizzying delights filled their eyes as they entered the elves' enormous dwelling place.

But not the least of the remarkable things about this village was the number of its inhabitants. From every corner, from behind benches and doorways, leaning over railings on the stairs and peering eagerly down from the balconies, hundreds of elves gazed back at him.

"Isn't this something?" Claus murmured to Anya.

"Did you hear that?" An elf whispered, delighted, from behind a nearby pillar. "He said it was 'something'!"

A second elf nodded eagerly. "He did, he did."

Dooley bustled forward to take his awestruck guests for his carefully planned tour. He guided them to an immense dining hall.

A tremendous kettle hung over the great firepit, its contents steaming and bubbling. An elf stood on a platform built around the caldron's lip, stirring, walking patiently around and around as he pushed an enormous spoon.

"That's Groot, our head cook," Dooley said, waving to him.

"Here, missus," Groot called. "You must be cold and hungry." He ladled a huge spoonful of stew into a bowl and leaned over the railing with it.

Anya ate a spoonful rather self-consciously, and swallowed. "Oh," she murmured, blinking. "It's very . . . um . . ." She glanced at Claus.

"Bland?" Patch said with a bit of a smirk.

"Bland, eh?" Groot shouted, his face reddening with anger as his oversensitive ears picked up the insult. "You try cooking for three hundred and forty-seven elves and see how much you can do!" His indignation began to rise, and so did his voice.

It was clearly an old wound. "Some want salt! Some want spice! Some want barley! Some want rice!"

"I was going to say it's very good," Anya called gently. Groot smiled, and his expression said that his heart was hers for life. Anya glanced at Patch with a smile that was equally warm, but still an admonition.

At last they circled back into the elf village's great central hall, where a spiral staircase led upward to an oddly oversized cottage perched like an aerie in the middle of the compound.

"What is it?" Claus asked.

Dooley puffed his chest with pride, spreading his arms. "*Your* house," he said.

"Our house?" Anya raised her hands to her cheeks in disbelief.

Dooley led the wondering couple up the spiral stairs and opened the solid wooden door of the house. Claus and Anya followed him inside wordlessly. Inside, the cottage was even more pleasant and cozy than Anya had imagined.

"Oh, it's sweet!" Anya said.

"Well, good people," Dooley said, ignoring their obvious puzzlement, "we'll leave you now to a good night's sleep."

Claus and Anya looked at each other now with expressions that bordered on panic. Patch moved away from Anya, hissing through his teeth, "Psst! Psst!"

"—What?" Dooley said, looking at him with a mixture of concern and exasperation.

"You forgot," Patch said, glancing toward the window.

"Forgot?" Dooley said.

"*You* know," Patch urged. He jerked his thumb at the window. "Toys," he mouthed. "Toys."

Dooley's eyes brightened at last. He nodded briskly, as he took his guests in hand once more. He led them across the Great Hall again, stopping this time before a set of massive wooden doors at its far side.

A great tunnel lay beyond the door, stretching for what seemed like miles, its far end lost from sight. From its walls and ceilings hung toys...countless fantastic, brightly painted toys in all shapes and sizes. "What are they?" Claus whispered at last, asking far more than just the question his words expressed.

"Christmas toys," Dooley raised his arms in a sweeping gesture. "You're going to deliver them. To all the children of the world."

Claus and Anya stared at him for a long moment. "But how can I deliver so many toys? It would take *years.*"

Dooley took a deep breath, and looked up at them again. "Both of you will live forever. Like us."

Claus lay beneath the eiderdown quilts of his comfortable new bed. He sighed heavily and changed position yet again. What was he, a simple woodcutter, doing in a place like this?

Dooley had finally explained that the elves had been making toys for human children for centuries, and leaving them where the children would find them. But as time passed, it grew more difficult and dangerous for the elves to venture too far into the human world; more and more of the toys they made could not be given out, and were left unused in their storeroom.

Then, one long-ago winter's night, the wisest elf of all, their venerable Ancient One, had a vision. He foretold that there would come a human who loved children as much as the elves did—who would become the one who would deliver their gifts for them to all the world.

They had been waiting—and preparing—for centuries for the day when the prophecy would come about. At last they had found, in Claus, its fulfillment.

Claus thought of Donner and Blitzen. He had not seen them since they had all entered the compound. If he was going to deliver toys, he needed his reindeer and sleigh. He slipped out from under the covers. Holding the lantern before him, he made his way tentatively down the spiral stairs and in the direction he remembered the elf taking as he led away the two reindeer.

At last he found the entrance to the stable. As he approached, he suddenly heard the voice of the elf Patch—speaking soothingly from somewhere inside:

"Easy boy. It's all right, easy now..."

The stable was a circular structure, with eight spacious stalls ringing its inner wall, facing center. At the far side of the room, Claus saw someone's sleeping quarters, complete with a bed. The name Patch was carved on the bed's footboard.

And in the stall nearest the bed, on the far side of the dimly lit circle, Donner stood, trembling with fright. Patch, dressed in a blue-and-white-striped nightshirt and cap, was standing beside him, speaking gently.

"Why don't you eat a little something, hmm?" Patch urged. "It's great food, believe me. See, look, even *I* like it. Yummm!"

Claus smiled, warming to this impulsive, unpredictable young elf. "He's like me, I guess," Claus said ruefully. "A little confused."

Startled, Patch spun around to face him. "Oh! I didn't—"

Claus started slowly across the creaking floor.

"He'll be just fine, sir," Patch said, with the assurance of someone who knew and loved animals. "He just needs a little elf-control." He grinned.

Claus smiled and nodded in agreement, glancing around at the other reindeer admiringly. "You certainly seem to know reindeer. These are fine specimens."

Patch straightened up proudly. "Hear that, boys?" he said to the reindeer. "You've made a good impression on your new boss."

"Boss? Me?" Claus said, raising his eyebrows.

Patch nodded. "Let me introduce you." He moved to the first two stalls. "Those two are twins," Patch said, "Prancer and Dancer. That's Comet, and the next one is Cupid. That one is Dasher," Patch said, moving on to the next stall. "And this noisy one here is Vixen."

"You sleep here?" Claus asked, both surprised and impressed that Patch should be so diligent in his care.

Patch nodded, pointing toward the one empty stall. "Over there," he said. "Where I do my other work," he added significantly. Draped over every available surface were elaborate blueprints, half-finished toy mockups, and odd random pieces of wood and leather.

"Sometimes I get so many ideas I don't know where to keep them in my head," Patch said enthusiastically. "One thing about me, I don't lack elf-assurance," he said, his grin widening.

The time flew by for Claus and Anya as they settled into their new life at the North Pole. They quickly grew to love the comfort—and the bustle—of their new home, the warm friendliness of the remarkable elves.

Meanwhile, Claus grew more and more familiar with the elves' workshops. They showed him their many skilled techniques for creating a seemingly endless supply of toys.

Claus also found himself gradually introduced to more inexplicable activities. By far one of the oddest things he was asked to do was to learn to drive a sleigh. He had protested that he was quite proficient at it already, but Dooley insisted that Claus had never driven a sleigh like *this* one. And when

Claus had been confronted by the curious arrangement of chairs, pulleys, and reins that Dooley presented to him, he had had to agree.

"Only a mockup," Dooley had assured him. "To simulate flight." He watched Claus cautiously for a reaction.

"Flight?" Claus echoed, his eyes widening in disbelief. "A flying sleigh?"

Dooley nodded. "Drawn by eight reindeer. Obviously we can't train you in the air on the real thing."

"Eight?" Claus repeated. He shook his head. That explained the other reindeer in the stable.

In the hours that followed, he discovered to his dismay how very little he knew about driving a sleigh—at least, a flying sleigh drawn by eight reindeer.

"Don't pull too hard or they'll bank too sharply," Dooley called out, standing to one side as Claus manipulated the mockup's reins. "Just a tug."

Claus let up on the reins, drew them in more slowly. "Now I'm climbing?"

"That's it," Dooley said, nodding, "but gently, gently. And always into the wind..."

Claus had thought the elves were tireless workers, but in the days and weeks that followed, their level of activity seem to increase a hundredfold.

Patch, being in charge of the reindeer stables, had no official role to play in the toymaking. But, never at a loss for ideas, and determined to make himself visible, he had decided that everyone worked more happily and efficiently to music. He loved music, and played the organ well, if he did say so himself. He gathered together a small band of other elves who were equally musically inclined, and set about making music while the others worked.

The success of Patch's music in improving the elves' productivity brought him new attention and many compliments, especially from Claus—and from the other elves, when they saw that Claus approved.

So, the elves began to initiate more of Patch's time-saving ideas. At his suggestion, the elves began working round-the-clock shifts, and in their dormitory he installed his new invention, the alarm clock.

As a result of his successful efficiency-oriented innovations, and because of Claus's respect for his skill, Patch was also given the plum project of designing a new sleigh to carry the toys on their Christmas journey. He was busier, and happier, than he had ever been in his life, now that his creativity had a positive outlet.

At last Christmas Eve arrived, and the final preparations for the Great Event began. An elf stood above a vast conveyor belt and, under Patch's careful supervision, poured the contents of a mysterious bag into a sieve, grinning with anticipation. As the contents spilled out and down, they appeared to be pure glittering stardust.

The mysterious dust drifted down and settled into the moving pile of feed, which began to glow and twinkle as if somehow transformed by the touch of magic.

Back in the stables, Patch and his assistants groomed the reindeer with extra care as the animals ate their ration of specially treated feed.

Claus went back to his quarters. After dinner he went into the bedroom to change.

"Northwest crosswind, point left to land. Southeast crosswind, point right...," he murmured. But no matter how often he thought about it, he still found it difficult to believe that he was actually going to be *flying* the sleigh tonight.

There was a knock at the door.

Claus looked up, all his nervousness instantly back again. Dooley stepped into the room, his normally cheerful face wearing a very serious expression. "It's time, sir."

"Oh," Claus said, swallowing the lump in his throat. "Right, right, coming..."

As Claus entered the tunnel with Anya and Dooley, a murmur spread through the crowd of waiting elves.

Claus moved out into the center of the tunnel to stand by his new sleigh; Anya took her place alongside Patch and Dooley at the front of the crowd, her cheeks flushed with delight. The crowd fell silent again, and for a long moment the vast room was filled with a breathless expectancy.

First came six elves who bore like a ceremonial train an immensely long beard, its ends neatly braided. As they emerged from the light, Claus saw that the beard belonged to a tremendously impressive and ancient-looking elf, who walked slowly and with great dignity behind them. Claus and Anya knew at once that this was the Ancient One, the elves' true spiritual leader, who had guided them in this selfless project.

"From this day on, now and forever, you will bring our gifts to all the children in all the world," the Ancient One spoke. "And all this is to be done on Christmas Eve." His voice rising strongly until it filled the hall, he proclaimed, "Let all within the sound of my voice and all who live on the earth know that you will be called... Santa Claus."

"Santa Claus," the elves echoed, all together, their voices hushed with awe.

Claus—Santa Claus—climbed into his waiting sleigh at last and blew a kiss to his wife.

The reindeer charged away down the tunnel; the beautiful hand-carved sleigh with its precious load flew forward as if it were shot out of a cannon, and sailed on through the star-filled sky. Santa Claus watched the team of eight reindeer galloping tirelessly ahead of him.

"Faster, boys!" he cried gleefully, having more fun than he had ever imagined was possible. "Feel the wind in your faces."

Santa Claus traveled in that one night far beyond any lands he had ever known, to places he had heard of only in legends and stories . . . and farther yet. And everywhere he left a gift for each child whose home he saw.

He returned to his North Pole home, to the jubilant elves and the welcoming arms of his wife.

And after that the weeks, months, and years passed with a magical rhythm that made them seem scarcely longer than days. And as the years went by, the world outside began, slowly but surely, to change. It was the Twentieth Century by now, and as technology—and the number of human beings—continued to grow with dizzying speed in the world outside, Santa Claus and his devoted helpers began to feel the strain on their traditional methods of production and delivery.

The elves stood waiting expectantly in the toy tunnel as Santa and his sleigh returned from yet another journey through the magical night before Christmas.

Patch checked the reindeer one by one, his face filled with concern. "Oh, boy, they look like they've been through the mill."

"Mill!" Santa said, a bit gruffly. "I can't remember the last time I saw a good old-fashioned mill. Now it's all apartment houses and skyscrapers. You think it's easy navigating through those skyscrapers? Not to mention the wind currents from those jumbo jets."

And in that other world, the world that a peasant couple named Claus and Anya had left centuries before, there was now a city called New York, on an island named Manhattan. The snow of the real world, cold and stinging, whirled past an elegant white mansion on a quiet side street in the Eighties on the Upper East Side.

A small boy about ten years old stepped out of a doorway. He pulled up the collar of his own coat—a torn and battered leather jacket, which he had found in a garbage can. Shivering, he pushed his mittenless, chill-reddened hands into his pockets.

His name was Joe. He had never known his father, and his mother had died more than a year ago. When the welfare people had come to take him to the orphanage, he had run away. Since then he had lived out on the streets, surviving however he could.

Joe had learned quickly to hide his feelings, to be suspicious of everyone. But beneath the tough manner of a boy old beyond his years was still a child who, wrapped in newspapers against the cold, sometimes cried himself to sleep at night, and dreamed of his mother's voice and her warm arms around him.

If he had known that he was being watched, he would never have let even a moment's longing show. But he did not know, and in the elegant townhouse across the street, silhouetted in a brightly lit window, someone stood staring out at him.

A young girl named Cornelia stood inside the tall bay windows, holding the curtains aside, gazing down at the ragged, shivering boy, who was just a little older than she. He looked so alone and sad. She knew that poor people lived near her home. She had even asked Miss Tucker, her nanny, to let her give some of her toys and clothes away; but Miss Tucker told her she was being very ungrateful and didn't deserve her stepuncle's kind generosity.

As Cornelia watched, the boy glanced up at her house. Her eyes met his dark, wary ones; he held her gaze for a moment that seemed to go on and on. And in that moment Cornelia felt as if a kind of electric shock tingled through her; in that moment she seemed to understand everything about him. She *knew* how lonely he must be.

Cornelia sighed, glancing reluctantly back into the living room as the high, nasal drone of Miss Tucker's voice intruded insistently on her private thoughts.

"I'm warning you, Cornelia; your stepuncle is not going to tolerate those grades. Imagine! A B-minus in geography!"

"What does he care about my marks?" Cornelia said with quiet defiance. "He never even looks at my report card. He probably doesn't even know what grade I'm in."

She blinked, and looked back out the window again. But across the street the doorway was empty; the boy was gone.

Back at the North Pole, Santa Claus's thoughts were centered at the moment more on streamlining his workload than on the injustices of the greater world beyond. He had called together Patch and Puffy, the two prime candidates for the newly announced position as his official Assistant.

"Your assistant!" Patch was saying, bright and breathless with excitement. "With all due respect, sir, I've got ideas that'll turn this place upside down! I'm talking about modern methods of production! I'm talking faster, quicker—"

"—and sloppier," Puffy interrupted skeptically.

Patch broke off, and turned to stare at his rival with undisguised disdain. "Just because *you* lack elf-assurance doesn't mean that I do, Puffy. I'm not afraid to rock the sleigh."

Puffy ignored him, keeping his own eyes on Santa Claus. Smiling ingratiatingly, he said, "Sir, I have long admired your traditional methods of manufacture. I assure you that I will give the same meticulous attention to quality and detail that—"

Santa held up his hands, cutting off the flow of verbiage.

"Boys, boys, don't give me campaign promises. Give me results. The one who gets the job is the one who does the job best."

During the next few weeks, the activity in the elves' vast factory was even more frantic than usual. But now the elf workers were pitted not against a deadline of Christmas Eve, but against each other.

Puffy continued to oversee the making of toys in the classic tradition of Santa's own exquisite handcrafted, hand-painted creations. He inspected each elf's work, giving all his attention to quality, even at the expense of quantity, just as Santa Claus had always done.

But at the same time, in the west wing of the factory, Patch and his handful of loyal friends were hard at work setting up a new, streamlined, fully automated production line. Guided by Patch's hastily drawn plans and inspired mechanical genius, it was ready to function in record time.

He lifted a hand, not for even a moment plagued by doubt over what he was about to do. "*Go!*" he cried.

The automatic toy-making machinery began to roll at top speed, and finished toys—shiny, new, and seemingly perfect—began to drop out at the other end, onto another belt, where they were swept off to be automatically sorted and stacked. *It worked!* Patch did a small dance of triumph.

But within the heart of Patch's ingenious machine, where no

elf or human eye could carefully watch over production, things were not functioning as intended. Patch's plans had been drawn up in too much of a hurry, and put together with too much haste. And so an automatic screwdriver, joining two parts of a bicycle frame together, did not turn the screws quite enough times to hold the pieces securely. A tiny red wagon had its handle attached—not quite tightly enough. Every toy that came tumbling off the conveyor belt had some fatal flaw hidden somewhere inside it, and yet every single toy coming off the line *looked* perfect.

All the elves of the village had gathered here to see who had won the competition. As Santa turned to look at them, Puffy's shoulders drooped. He could see for himself, just as clearly as everyone else assembled there could see, that Patch had won the contest.

The Manhattan street was bright with tinsel and colored lights. Shoppers hurried by, their arms full of Christmas gifts, as Joe stood outside the window of Cornelia's townhouse, peeking through the glass at the warm, well-lit room and the heavily laden table.

Cornelia started as she saw the face of the young boy she had watched standing alone on the street a few weeks before, his brown eyes wide and his thin face filled with longing. But as he looked along the table, he suddenly found her looking back at him. Quickly he ducked down out of sight.

Cornelia opened the back door. Peering out into the darkness, she called softly, "*Psst!* Little boy?"

She held a plate of food out before her in the glow of the porch light. Then, very carefully and in plain sight, she set it down on the steps. She turned and went back into the house.

Out in the shrubbery behind the house, Joe grinned, for the first time in days, as he gulped down the first real meal he had eaten in longer than he could remember. Roast beef and gravy was absolutely heavenly.

Happy and utterly unsuspecting that countless toys within his bag had hidden flaws, Santa Claus guided his team and sleigh out of the tunnel ramp and into the sky for one more Christmas Eve trip.

"Ah, what a night, my boys, what a night!" Santa cried to his team as the sleigh circled the skyscrapers of New York City. "Look down there—" Santa gestured with a mittened hand at the scene below. "Tonight there isn't a child alive who isn't bursting with joy and happiness and—" He broke off, as he saw something down below that rang discordantly with his merry vision.

In an alley below, a young boy was huddled all alone by a garbage can bonfire, shivering with cold. "Just a minute, boys," Santa said, "I think we're going to make an unscheduled stop."

The sleigh landed silently on the roof of a tenement just above the street where the boy was.

Joe stepped back inside the tenement's doorway, escaping another gust of icy wind. He looked up in surprise as a large, bulky shape materialized abruptly beside him in the doorway. "Hey!" he said, anger covering his fright. "Beat it, man. Find your own doorway. Don't crowd me."

The fat old man in the red suit said gently, "Don't you know who I am?"

Joe shrugged. "Sure. You're a nut."

"I'm Santa Claus," the old man said, patting his well-padded front.

"Right." Joe put his hands on his hips. "And I'm the Tooth Fairy."

"I'll prove it to you," Santa Claus said almost desperately. He held out his hand. "Come up on the roof with me."

"No way, man," Joe said. "You get outta here or I call a cop."

"Oh, you poor lad," Santa murmured. He folded his arms. "Well, I see I'm going to have to do it my way."

One moment Joe had been standing in a doorway. And then he found himself suddenly and completely inexplicably standing on a rooftop, with the same crazy old man still beside him. "Holy cow!" he cried.

"How about a ride?" said Santa.

"On *that?*" Joe pointed at the sleigh. His mouth dropped open.

"Make up your mind," Santa said, showing just the slightest trace of restlessness. "I'm in kind of a hurry tonight."

"I mean, yeah, sure...."

Santa led him to the sleigh and helped him climb up into its seat. "Hold on tight now," Santa said. "Don't worry, you're as safe here as you would be at home."

"I ain't got a home," Joe said bluntly, as reality pushed its ugly face into his wonderful, magical dream.

Joe let out a yelp of startled delight as the sleigh swooped upward, just clearing the top of a skyscraper.

Santa Claus nodded. "It's not too hard. Here—take the reins." He passed them into Joe's wondering hands. And then, just as he had done in dreams for countless years, for a son he had never had, Santa Claus began to teach Joe how to handle the sleigh and team.

"Where are we goin'?" Joe asked.

"We can't joy-ride all night," Santa said good-naturedly. "I've got a job to do, you know." He took the reins out of Joe's reluctant hands again, guiding the reindeer down to a precise landing on a dark rooftop.

Cornelia lay in her large, soft bed, as weariness finally overcame her excited Christmas Eve anticipation. Suddenly, a crash sounded somewhere in the townhouse. She threw back her covers, tiptoed down the hall and into the darkened living room.

Santa and Joe spun around together, caught in the act of delivering presents.

"Are you him?" Cornelia gasped, amazed. "Are you Santa Claus?"

"Oh boy, I hate it when this happens," Santa muttered under his breath. Putting a broad smile on his face, he said, "Hello, little girl."

Cornelia pointed at the new present among the others heaped up beneath the tree. "Is that my dolly?" Her eyes flickered up again as Joe helped Santa set a red-and-green package under the tree. "It's you," she cried.

Joe really looked at the girl for the first time, and realized that he knew her, too. *"You?"* he asked incredulously. It was the red-haired girl who had left dinner out for him on several different nights during the past few weeks.

"You two know each other?" Santa asked, equally surprised.

Joe and Cornelia stared at each other, frozen in fascination, face to face at last after so much time.

"I'm . . . Cornelia." Cornelia glanced down, suddenly shy.

"I'm Joe," Joe said, pushing his hands into his pockets, equally self-conscious.

She looked up at Joe from under her eyelashes, suddenly shy again. He was the bravest and handsomest boy she had ever seen, she thought—and he certainly knew the most wonderful people!

Joe looked back at her, blushing slightly. "Hey, um, Cor . . ." Joe hesitated. "What's your name again?"

"Cornelia," she said.

"That's too fancy," Joe said, frowning to cover the fact that he had trouble pronouncing it. "I'll call you Corny."

She looked up again, grinning with delight.

Santa was gathering up his sack of presents. Joe glanced toward him, and Cornelia realized that they were both about to leave. "I can make you a bowl of ice cream," she said hastily, knowing Santa could not stay, but wanting Joe to, desperately.

"Well . . ." Joe licked his lips, glancing back at Santa, torn.

Santa Claus smiled, seeing his dilemma and quickly offering him a way out. "I'll tell you what, Joe. You stay and have something to eat. I'll see you again." He realized, a bit relieved, that it would make parting much easier for both of them this way.

"You will? You mean it?" Joe demanded, both yearning and dismayed.

Santa nodded. "Santa Claus doesn't lie, Joe. Next Christmas Eve, we've got a date. Okay?"

Joe grinned. "You bet!"

With a farewell wave, Santa took a deep breath and vanished from sight.

Christmas Day dawned bright and cold over the great metropolis of New York, and, hour by hour, all around the world, boys and girls everywhere were waking up and opening their presents from Santa, and rushing outside to play with them. And, one after another, finding that the toys which had looked so shiny and perfect were actually a fraud, ready to fall apart in their hands. Patch's sloppy manufacturing methods were dealing Santa Claus's reputation a terrible, painful blow.

Dooley sat in his easy chair late one evening a few days after Christmas, peacefully reading. A sudden clatter and crash coming down his chimney sent him leaping up from his seat, as several dozen broken toys came hurtling down the chimney to land in a great heap in his fireplace. Clutching the appalling evidence of a genuine crisis, he hurried out into the compound, and ordered the nearest elf to go in search of Patch.

Then, carrying the load of broken pieces, Dooley went to report to Santa Claus.

"Returns!" Claus cried in horrified dismay, as Dooley stood in his living room and held the ruined toys out to him. "We've *never* had returns."

Anya sat in her chair by the fire, stunned, too upset even to speak.

A timid rapping at the front door made them all turn as one. Patch stood there, his face a mask of cheerful greeting, but there was a dark, haunted gleam in his eyes.

"Oh," Claus said, as Patch entered the room.

"Hi there," Patch said feebly.

The awkwardness of the situation was so thick that Anya could have cut it with a knife.

"I'm sure you had no idea—" Claus forced the words out, knowing they must both acknowledge the grave seriousness of the situation, and sensing that Patch was unwilling, or unable, to do it. He wiped unaccustomed perspiration from his brow. "Patch, how can I say this?"

Before he could say the words Patch dreaded to hear, the elf interrupted again, frantically. "Can we have a man-to-elf talk here?" As he spoke, he untied his bright red Assistant's apron with fumbling hands, and began to take it off.

"I just feel that red really isn't my color," Patch rattled. "It just doesn't suit my . . . um . . . complexion." His eyes pleaded for forgiveness, for a sign that Santa truly understood.

"No, no, I'll take it," Claus said hastily. And before he lost his own resolution, he took the apron from Patch's hand; turning away, he hurried to the cottage door, closing it abruptly behind him.

At last Anya, still standing beside Patch in the silent room, asked softly, "Will you be all right?"

Patch pulled himself together with an effort, and grinned with false bravado. "Me? I couldn't be happier."

Whistling a shaky little tune, he turned and hurried out of Santa's home.

Late that night, when all the elf village lay asleep, Patch crept out of his refuge in the stable and stepped out into the snow. He carried a single bundle slung over his shoulder on a stick as he left his home like a fugitive, without a single good-bye.

The sack slung over his shoulder glittered softly with its own light. It was not the bag of belongings he had originally intended to take with him. Instead it was the bag of magic stardust that he added to the reindeer's feed every year.

"I'll show him what I'm made of," he muttered. "I'll make him take notice, I will."

The Capitol Building lay as serenely white as the snow-covered lawns and trees of Washington, D.C. The city rested peacefully on a crisp, blue-skied winter day shortly after the New Year.

Within the halls of the Capitol, the minds of the eight U.S. Senate Subcommittee members seated at the long curving table were still on the recent holidays—but not on thoughts of good cheer. The press, television crews, miscellaneous aides, and a gallery full of spectators filled the vast chamber, all watching and listening with great intentness as the investigation's key figure began his testimony at last. The defendant in this particular instance was none other than the president of the B.Z. Toy Company, one of the largest toymakers in the nation.

B.Z. himself was now answering questions about the highly questionable business practices of the company he headed.

"Now, sir," the chairman said, his voice rising in righteous

anger, "I am asking you if this toy is manufactured by your company."

"... Uh, it appears to be our product, Senator," B.Z. said, glancing at the toy suspiciously.

An aide stepped up to the table next to the evidence—a sweet-faced doll in a frilly pink gown. He set an ashtray containing a lit cigarette next to the doll. Within seconds, the doll's flimsy, highly flammable dress began to smoke, and suddenly burst into flames.

"What do you say to *that,* sir?" the chairman asked, his eyes blazing with the fire of his outrage.

B.Z. pulled at the collar of his neat white shirt, "Well, Senator, I always knew smoking was dangerous. Heh, heh..."

But the senators were plainly not amused. "This is not a laughing matter, sir!" the chairman said sharply. "This is a tragedy waiting to happen."

B.Z. looked back at the chairman again, wiping his face. "I'll make sure it never occurs again."

"You'd better do more than that, sir," the chairman snapped to B.Z. "You'd better recall every B.Z. Toy on the market, or I'll personally see to it that your license to manufacture and distribute in the United States is revoked."

B.Z. mopped his brow again with his already sodden linen handkerchief. "Senator, may I—" he whined.

"Next witness!" the chairman called, his gaze still fixed dramatically on the crowd.

At the same time, in a spot unmarked on any map, Santa Claus rested his head in his hands. "Patch gone, and it's all my—"

"It's *not* your fault," Anya said, gently but with absolute belief.

"Where will he go? What will he do?" Santa Claus said. He wished that someday the small, impulsive genius would find his way back to his rightful home and the people who loved him.

But Patch had no intention of returning to the home he had abandoned, at least not until they admitted to what he still saw as their mistake. And so, not many days later, the most impulsive of elves found himself walking quite confidently down a street in midtown Manhattan, studying the windows of department stores with frank fascination.

He stopped short in his wanderings, as something in a store window suddenly caught his eye. Beneath a banner bearing a distinctive logo and the slogan B.Z. TOYS—FOR HAPPY GIRLS AND BOYS was a vast assortment of toys, stuffed animals, and dolls. As he watched, a clerk began systematically to sweep them from the display window in armloads and carry them away. Patch watched in amazement, astonished to think of how wonderful a line of toys must be to be disappearing so rapidly. He turned to the nearest human on the street. "They must be very popular," he said, pointing at the toys. "Look at how fast they're selling."

At the same moment B.Z. was brooding in his townhouse not terribly far away. He knew that a financial disaster of major proportions was already in the process of occurring at the B.Z. Toy Company.

So, despite his depressing lack of inspiration, he boarded his private helicopter and flew out to his company headquarters on Long Island.

B.Z. settled into the wide, leather-upholstered back seat of the limousine waiting for him at the airport. Also waiting for him, with all the enthusiasm of a condemned man awaiting the executioner, was his chief assistant and Head of Research and Development, Dr. Eric Towzer.

"Okay, Towzer," B.Z. said grimly. "Give it to me straight."

Towzer squirmed and tugged at his collar. "The retail outlets are pulling our toys off the shelves so fast you'd think they were disease carriers."

"Cowards," B.Z. muttered, disgusted.

When the limousine drove up and stopped before the office building, B.Z. launched himself from it and entered the offices like a charging rhino. "Miss Abruzzi!" he roared, as he neared his secretary's desk, just outside his office.

"Yes, B.Z.?" Miss Abruzzi chirped, instantly on the alert.

"No calls!" B.Z. stormed, in passing. "No visitors!" He slammed the door to his office so hard behind him that the pictures on the wall rattled and swayed.

As B.Z. entered his private sanctuary a voice said suddenly and quite distinctly, "Keeping banker's hours, eh? I thought you'd never get here."

The leather chair swiveled around.

B.Z. stopped short, gaping in disbelief. There, smiling confidently and even putting feet shod in pointy-toed boots up on *his* desk top, was an apparition out of one of his catalogues, a toy elf come to life.

"What are you?" B.Z. bellowed, losing all patience.

Patch shrugged. "Isn't it elf-explanatory?" He gestured down at himself, at his colorful clothes, with a sweeping gesture.

"Why are you here?" B.Z. asked, trying desperately to ask a question which would elicit a rational response.

Patch brightened, and smiled again. "I gather you're a great toy-giver. I'm a great toy-maker. We should get together."

"Why would I do that?" B.Z. growled, instantly suspicious.

"Well, you know the old saying—" Patch said whimsically. "Heaven helps those who help their elf. Just let me use your toy factory," he said, his eyes shining with sudden eagerness.

"To make what?" B.Z. asked bluntly.

Patch grinned. "Something special. Here's the idea. First you stop making all your regular toys. We won't need them anymore."

B.Z. brightened, his own eyes lighting up at the prospect of something—anything—that would replace his own suddenly notorious and unsellable line.

"Tell me something," the elf said, his face suddenly pulling down with a frown of concern. "You're a man of the world and I'm just an elf of the top-of-the-world. How can we tell all the people about my 'something special'?"

B.Z. grinned. "Advertise," he said simply. "In my line, television works best." His mind began to turn over the possibilities for a new ad campaign to restore his tarnished image.

Patch nodded suddenly. "Oh," he said. "Those little picture-box thingies? Can we get on those?"

B.Z. snorted. "With money, a horse in a hoopskirt can get on television. So when?"

"Christmas Eve."

"How much will this cost?" B.Z. snapped, asking the one thing he really wanted to know, at last.

"Cost?" Patch said blankly. "Cost who?"

"The people who buy the toys," B.Z. answered impatiently.

"Oh, nothing." Patch said blithely. "We're going to give it away free."

B.Z. sputtered inarticulately. Spitting out the words that were choking him, he wheezed, "*Give* something away? For *free??*"

Patch nodded. "That's how we do it at the North Pole."

B.Z. rubbed his chin thoughtfully. "Hmm," he murmured. "This *would* go a long way to cleaning up my public image." B.Z. took a deep breath. "This . . . product you say they'll all want. What is it?"

Patch smiled again. "It's cheap. It's simple. And it's got a secret ingredient." He held out his hand. In his palm lay a few precious grains of the magical reindeer fodder, glinting like captive stars.

It was a balmy summer's day on Long Island as B.Z. strolled across the grounds of his Toy Company toward the one factory building that was not locked up tight. Dr. Towzer followed faithfully behind him, perspiring, toting a padlocked briefcase.

This was the first time in weeks he had even dared to intrude on the elf's work area. But now at last they had the samples he had requested.

"Yes?" Patch said, a trifle impatiently.

"We've brought the prototypes for . . . *it*," B.Z. said almost diffidently. He gestured to Towzer, who handed him the briefcase. He opened it. Inside, resting on a velvet cushion, were four lollipops: a round one, a long thin one, a big all-day sucker, and a very small one.

"That one," Patch said, pointing at the small one.

"What color?" Towzer asked.

Patch shrugged. "What color do you like?"

"I like puce," Towzer said eagerly.

Patch nodded. "Fine, puce then," he said brusquely. Without another word, he shut the door in their faces.

Back at the North Pole, Santa Claus sat in his rocking chair before the fire, whittling pensively at a block of wood.

"Oh my! An elf-portrait!" Anya said, her voice betraying her amazement as she saw what her husband was doing.

"It's for Joe," Claus said softly, expressing his inner thoughts with hesitant difficulty. "He makes me think what our son would have been like."

Anya took the wooden elf from him, looking at it more closely. "Why, it's Patch!"

"My good old Patch," Claus murmured. "I hope he's all right."

Patch stood in the middle of a television studio, clad in an *haute couture* version of the elf attire which had been personally designed for him: an immaculately cut, styled—and then sequin-covered—version of his old clothing, this time made entirely of patchwork squares in vibrant puce and blue.

"I don't know about this," he muttered weakly. "It isn't what the North Pole looks like at all."

All around him lay a display of almost mind-boggling bad taste and vulgarity.

"Look," Towzer said reassuringly, "B.Z. knows how to grab the people."

"Places, everybody," the floor manager's voice called.

Patch stood frozen where he was, like a bug in a spotlight, as offstage the announcer's voice began its introductory spiel: "Live! From New York! Presenting . . . direct from the North Pole, that perky pixie, PATCH!"

But the words of merry greeting which he had rehearsed for days now seemed completely unfamiliar to him. First they crawled by so slowly that he had to drag out every word as if he were talking through a mouthful of glue; then they abruptly speeded up until his tongue had to run full tilt to follow.

Across the United States parents and children glanced up from their tree-trimming and present-wrapping to see the odd apparition in the glitzy patchwork suit smile and recite ingratiatingly,

"From the Old North Pole
Where elves make toys,
Here's a Christmas treat
For you girls and boys!
Oh, my name is Patch
And as you can tell,
I'm an elf myself,
So let's give a yell!"

The bizarre spectacle circled the world as B.Z. had promised, bouncing from satellite to satellite, emerging in countless languages from television sets wherever they might be....

Even at the North Pole.

In the elves' compound Dooley, Gooba, and Puffy sat together in the information center of Dooley's quarters, watching the brightly painted picture box. Their faces turned pale and tight-lipped with shocked dismay as the garish display went on and on, and Patch's obvious Christmas Eve competition with Santa Claus began to take awful shape.

Dooley raised his hand. "Quick," he said to Puffy. "Get Santa Claus in here right now."

Back in New York City, in the living room of her townhouse, Cornelia shook her head. The ghastly commercial sat as uncomfortably in the pit of her stomach as the TV dinner. Just then Miss Tucker entered the living room. Cornelia glanced up at her.

"Cornelia," Miss Tucker called, "your stepuncle has stopped by for a minute. Go in and wish him a Merry Christmas."

Cornelia rose distractedly from the sofa and followed her nanny to the library.

"Merry Christmas, Uncle," Cornelia said politely.

B.Z. swiveled around in his seat and stared in surprise at his waiting stepniece. Then he grinned, flushed with triumph at having just pulled off the greatest promotional gimmick he—

or anyone else—had ever dreamed up. Merry Christmas? He chuckled. "It certainly should be," he said cheerfully.

Later on Christmas Eve, B.Z., Grizzard his chauffeur, and Miss Abruzzi watched eagerly as Patch turned on the ignition of his new "delivery system"—the Patchmobile. This was Patch's answer to Santa's sleigh and reindeer. It was the ultimate in modern rocket technology.

The Patchmobile roared forward up the lighted ramp, crossing the distance to the open doorway in a matter of heart beats—launching upward into the night.

"He did it!" B.Z. shouted exultantly. "That little son-of-a-gun!"

Leaning on his horn exultantly, Patch laughed in giddy glee as he roared between the starry towers of Manhattan to the strains of his very own Christmas theme.

Santa Claus journeyed fast and far that night. But Patch, in his rocket car, was always faster. Struggling to keep his flagging spirits up, Santa looked down across the nighttime landscape of Manhattan, which had always filled him with such pleasure. A motion his subconscious had been searching for all along registered in his thoughts. Abruptly his smile came back, as wide as ever. "Ah," he sighed. "At least somebody down there likes me."

Far below him stood the small form of the boy Joe, waving wildly at him from the roof of a tenement.

Santa shifted the reins, and the eight reindeer began to circle downward as one, to come in for a perfect landing on the rooftop below.

"Coming?" he called to the breathlessly waiting boy.

"Neat!" Joe cried.

He scrambled up into the sleigh besides Santa and settled himself comfortably in the seat.

Santa reached down and handed Joe the special handmade present. "For me?" Joe whispered. "A present?"

"Yup," Santa said, smiling gently.

Joe unwrapped the red-and-green paper with clumsy haste, revealing the carved figure of an elf. It was the first Christmas present he had received since running away from the orphanage.

"Excellent!" he said with a grin, unconsciously echoing Cornelia's favorite expression. "Thanks!" He held Santa's gaze for a long moment. "Did Corny get something?"

Santa grinned. "Writes a lovely letter, that girl. Asked for a toy piano."

The next morning dawned clear and crisp over the Big Apple and its sprawling suburbs. Children awoke and came running to discover what surprises had been left for them beneath their Christmas trees.

In one sunny home in Queens, a blond tousle-headed little boy ran to the Christmas tree and seized the small patchwork present that waited there, ignoring everything else.

It was the most wonderful lollipop he had ever seen, for it seemed to glow all by itself, like the lights on the tree. At its center was the magical dust that was meant to enchant the feed of Santa's own reindeer. The little boy took one step and then another as he ate the pop, beginning to wander toward the other packages under the tree. But as he took another step, something remarkable began to happen to him: He began to rise up into the air. He hovered halfway to the ceiling, his mouth stretched wide into a smile of pure delight. The Patch present let him walk on air!

In only one home in all of New York City did the patchwork present lie unopened beneath the tree. Cornelia sat on the thick rug in the den, picking out the tune to "Jingle Bells" on her new toy piano, letting the melody conjure up for her the image of Santa's merry, smiling face.

Miss Tucker stood on the other side of the angel-hair-bedecked Christmas tree, holding Patch's gift out to her with impatient curiosity. "But don't you even want to try it?" she insisted.

"I certainly do *not,*" Cornelia said adamantly.

Miss Tucker looked at the present with longing. "Well . . . ," she said hesitantly, "it seems a shame to let it go to waste. Do you mind if I take it?" she asked at last.

Cornelia didn't even bother to look up. "I don't care," she said.

Miss Tucker crunched the lollipop with her strong horselike teeth, licking her lips.

And then the magic began to happen with a vengeance. Like a hot air balloon in the Macy's parade, Miss Tucker began to drift up from the floor. "*Whooo!*" she gasped, clutching her head in astonishment.

Cornelia stared in open disbelief as Miss Tucker began to flap her arms like wings, scooting across the room like a ponderous hen trying to stay airborne. "Ooohh," she shrilled, laughing giddily for the first time either she or Cornelia could remember. "Look at me! I feel just like Mary Poppins!"

B.Z. leaned easily against his raised desk, glancing around his crowded office. The large room was packed wall to wall with reporters, photographers, and television camera crews, all eager to get the story on the elf who had scooped Santa Claus—and his magnanimous sponsor.

B.Z. said grandly, "Boys, let me tell you—I owe all this good fortune to me, my elf, and I!"

But not everyone in the room smiled; not everyone there had as short a memory as B.Z. liked to hope the American public did.

"What about the fact that the Senate Subcommittee on Toy Safety cited this company for fifteen separate violations of—"

B.Z.'s mouth snapped shut, his toothy grin disappearing. "Okay, ladies and gentlemen, that's it for now."

As the last reporter was pushed rather unceremoniously out the doors, B.Z. remained behind with only Patch beside him. Patch looked up at the toy manufacturer, his face troubled. "What was that about a Senate Subcommittee?" He wasn't quite certain what that was, but he understood "toy safety" and "violations" well enough.

"That's just typical newspaper garbage. Silly stuff . . . the future is ours, Patch!" B.Z. said heartily.

"But I'm going back to the North Pole," Patch protested. "Now that I've shown Santa Claus what I can do, it's for sure he'll send for me to come home."

B.Z. rubbed his chin, thinking furiously. He didn't really need the elf any more—just that secret ingredient. He smiled like a barracuda about to swallow a minnow. "This reindeer cornflakes, whatever it is that makes the kids float on air—what would happen if you, er, made it stronger?"

"Why, it's elf-explanatory," Patch shrugged. "It would make them fly."

"Could you do that? Before you go?"

"Lollipops?" Patch asked.

B.Z. shook his head emphatically. "No. The consumer always wants a new model."

"Candy canes?"

B.Z.'s mouth stretched into a broad smile again. "Candy canes! Patch, you are some terrific elf!"

Patch sat behind the controls of his state-of-the-art control panel, overseeing the endless metal forest of robotic arms and automated machinery which produced more candy canes in an hour than he could have imagined producing in his wildest dreams.

He knew he was very unhappy. He missed Santa more than

he had ever dreamed possible. He *had* been elfish, he realized, thinking only of personal glory.

Beyond the factory walls a cold, hard winter rain was drenching New York. Soaked to the skin in spite of his best efforts at keeping dry, Joe scurried toward Cornelia's townhouse. He crept across the backyard and around to the side of the building. Picking up a pebble, he took careful aim and tossed it against an upper window.

Cornelia came to the window and pushed it open.

"Hi," Joe said, his nonchalant pose ruined by a loud, sudden sneeze.

"Come up, quick," Cornelia whispered loudly.

Startled by the invitation, but hoping for it all along, Joe didn't wait to be asked twice.

He shinnied up the drainpipe and climbed in over the sill, to stand wonderingly in her actual room like a very young Romeo inside Juliet's house at last.

She gestured at the cold, rainy night beyond her window. "You're staying here."

"I'm what?" Joe said in disbelief.

Cornelia's eyes shone with fresh excitement and sudden inspiration. "There's an empty room in the basement near the furnace room. I'm going down and fix it up for you."

She bustled out of the room with an armful of blankets.

On the same frigid, rainy night, another surreptitious figure made its way up the street to B.Z.'s townhouse and knocked on his door.

Dr. Towzer stood on his doorstep, looking like a drowned spaniel.

"Good grief, man!" B.Z. stared at him in astonishment. "Haven't you ever heard of the telephone?"

"I didn't *dare* use the telephone, B.Z. I couldn't take a chance of anyone hearing!"

Down in the basement Cornelia was sitting on the floor in her bathrobe, next to Joe's makeshift bed. She removed the thermometer gently from Joe's mouth, and read his temperature.

"Ninety-nine. You still have a temperature." Cornelia said, in her best efficient nurse's tone. "Vitamin C, that's what you need. Come on, let's get some orange juice."

They started up the cellar steps, but as they reached the top of the stairs, Cornelia froze, motioning for Joe to stop too, hearing men's voices coming through the door.

In the kitchen B.Z. poured himself a drink and filled a glass for Towzer. He smiled, a smile that Attila the Hun would have appreciated. "*Santa Claus is finished!* I'm taking over Christmas," he cried.

Joe and Cornelia stood motionless, holding their breath. And then suddenly Cornelia saw a new kind of horror fill Joe's face. His nose twitched, and his mouth popped open as he inhaled sharply.

"*Ah-choo!*" Joe sneezed resoundingly.

B.Z. leaped to his feet. "What the—" he cried in sudden fury.

Joe pushed Cornelia ahead of him as they reached the bottom of the stairs, shoving her into the only hiding place he could immediately spot, behind the wine racks.

B.Z. roared down the stairs, and was on top of the petrified boy before he could move, grabbing him by the collar and dragging him back up the steps into the kitchen.

"Who are you? How'd you get in here?"

Joe, recovering from his initial fright at being captured, began to kick and struggle, lashing out at his captor with all the streetwise moves he knew.

Frantic at their discovery, Towzer rushed to the back door and whistled loudly. A moment later Grizzard, massive and menacing, appeared in the doorway in answer to his summons.

Joe twisted desperately in B.Z.'s grasp, making a final, frantic

effort to break free. He found the toy mogul's hand on his shoulder and bit down on it as hard as he could.

B.Z. howled with pain.

Joe wriggled free as B.Z. lost his grip, and tried to run, but Grizzard caught the boy in a painful, viselike grip. "Who is this kid?" he asked.

"Some little sneak thief—" B.Z. snarled, sucking on his wounded hand.

"I heard what you said!" Joe cried defiantly. "You ain't never gonna beat Santa Claus. *Never!* I'll tell him and he'll beat you, he'll get his guys—"

B.Z.'s eyes narrowed ominously; he glared at Joe with sudden suspicion. Was this kid more than he seemed? Could this Santa Claus actually have planted a kid in his house as a spy?

Grizzard carried the helplessly struggling boy out to B.Z.'s waiting limousine, and locked him in its trunk. B.Z. watched in satisfaction as the long black car drove off into the night, heading for his factory. He shook his head, taking a long swig of his drink to calm his frayed nerves.

"First some kid in my basement and then you come waltzing in my house in the middle of the night and—" He broke off, staring at Towzer as if he had only just noticed him. "Hey, yeah, Towzer, what do *you* want, anyway?" he snapped.

Towzer took a deep breath, lips trembling as he forced the bad news out between them: "It's the candy canes. I had to move one of the batches of them to another part of the factory. I left one box next to a radiator in the lab."

"And?" B.Z. bellowed.

"The candy canes exploded!" Towzer cried. "They react to extreme heat and turn volatile! This stuff can kill people!"

B.Z. sneered. "Are you going soft on me? There has to be some way to get around this nasty little complication...."

Cornelia pushed open the dumbwaiter doors as they disappeared from the room, tiptoed down the hall past the half-open door, and crept silently back up the stairs to her bedroom.

Patch lay in his bed in the empty B.Z. Toy Company factory, enjoying the peace and quiet of the silent night, totally unaware that it was only the calm before a terrible storm.

Grizzard dragged Joe down the black, echoing stairwell into the subbasement of the factory where, unknown to him, Patch had his secret store of magic dust hidden. Unconcerned, Grizzard bound Joe's hands and feet to a water pipe, completing his imprisonment. "Listen, kid," he rasped, "if you wanna die on me while I'm gone, be my guest."

Waking to a new day, Cornelia leaped from her bed. She sat down and began to scribble the words she had composed last night as quickly as her hand would form the letters:

"Dear Santa. You've got to help right away. Joe has been taken prisoner by a very bad man, and..."

Her head came up in sudden fright as her bedroom door was flung open. Miss Tucker stood there with her stepuncle glowering in the background.

"Cornelia!" Miss Tucker said sharply. "What are you doing? You're ten minutes late for breakfast!"

The letter lay where she had left it on the desk in the quiet room, when a gentle breeze began to stir the air. The magical breeze, which searched the world each day for letters like hers, cupped the letter in its invisible hands, lifting it gently from the tabletop and carrying it up the chimney.

Santa stared in surprise as he actually saw a letter drop down his chimney and sweep past the flames to land on the hearth all alone. He stared at the curious message written on the envelope: EMERGENCY! OPEN IMMEDIATELY!

"It's Joe!" he cried ripping open the envelope. "Hitch up the reindeer."

Cornelia paced restlessly about her bedroom. Suddenly a great *whoosh* filled the hearth of her fireplace with a cloud of ashes, and Santa Claus stood smiling before her.

"*Where* is Joe?" Santa said.

Cornelia's hands made fists. "My stepuncle's got him." But I must tell you something else. Those candy canes..."

Santa was already gesturing her toward the chimney. "Tell me on the way." He swept her into the circle of his magic spell, and, touching the side of his nose, transported them to the roof and his waiting sleigh.

As they headed toward the toy factory, Cornelia breathlessly explained to Santa all that had happened.

"They exploded?" Santa asked, aghast.

She nodded. "I called the police, but I don't think they believed me."

Santa's face grew even grimmer. "We haven't a second to lose."

Patch sat at his control board, as the robot machines made their endless candy canes. Suddenly the buzzer sounded as the stardust hopper's gauge registered empty. Patch roused himself from his seat and clattered down the metal staircase to the dark subcellar.

Patch suddenly stopped short as a small, muted sound registered in his ears. It sounded like...someone crying?

At last, rounding a large rusty trash bin, he found its source: a young boy, bound and gagged, tied to a pipe.

He knelt down and with fumbling hands started to untie Joe's hands and feet, stopping only to remove the gag from the boy's mouth. "What are you doing down here?" Patch asked.

"As if you didn't know, creep," the boy said bitterly, his reddened eyes blazing.

Patch sat back, his astonishment complete. *"Me?"* he asked.

"You're the one," the boy said furiously, tears of helpless anger still running down his cheeks. "You ruined Christmas."

"I never did!" Patch said indignantly.

"Santa said I was his only friend left, ya dumb punk!"

Patch froze, his anger draining away as he realized that the weeping boy was really serious. His heart sank. Had his plan to win back Santa's love and respect truly backfired so completely?

All the wild fury that had been trapped inside Joe during his ordeal spilled over as he saw what he took to be Patch's silent indifference; he lunged forward and began to punch and pummel the elf.

"He saw what you are—a stink-face creep who made kids hate the best guy that ever—" As they struggled together, something dropped from the boy's pocket. It was a bright wooden toy of a kind very familiar to Patch's trained eye.

He moved away from Joe, their fight forgotten as he bent down to pick it up. He saw that it was a carved wooden elf, its face a perfect re-creation of his own. "He *does* like me after all."

His mind racing, Patch fitted pieces of a new plan together with lightning speed.

"Come on, kid!" he cried, gesturing to Joe.

"Where we going," Joe called.

"The North Pole," Patch said decisively. "And for once, we'll bring *Santa Claus* a present."

Patch led him through the factory to the vast storeroom, where a glowing mountain of magic candy lay at the foot of a huge chute. "There's enough here to take care of all next year's Christmas orders. Santa Claus can take a year off."

Santa's sleigh soared over the wintry suburbs of Long Island. With Cornelia's sure guidance, they were closing in rapidly on the B.Z. Toy Company factory.

Not so very far away, inside the factory, Patch and Joe had just finished loading the huge mountain of candy canes into the back of the Patchmobile. At last Patch climbed into the driver's seat, and motioned to Joe to join him.

"Fasten your seat belt," he instructed.

The Patchmobile charged up the runway and soared out through the open hangar doors, rocketing away into the ozone.

Santa and Cornelia looked down over the side of the sleigh to see the rocketing Patchmobile.

"It's them," Cornelia cried, pointing ahead.

Santa's own wide stare of surprise suddenly changed to a look of fear. *"Oh, no!"* he cried.

"The candy canes! They're in the car with them!"

Desperately, Santa shouted to his reindeer, *"Faster! Faster! Come on boys, fly like the wind!"*

And inside the Patchmobile's trunk, where no one could see what was about to happen next, a stress crack opened in the Patchmobile's framework, revealing unprotected wiring. Another wrenching dive tore the wires apart. A spark flickered, and then another, as the short-circuiting wires began to sizzle.

Fat Blitzen's tongue was lolling in his mouth, the reindeer's heaving flanks were white with foam from their exertion, but slowly, slowly, the sleigh was gaining on the cavorting Patchmobile.

"Come on, boys!" Santa shook the reins. "It's Patch in there!"

At last even Patch and Joe were suddenly, frighteningly aware that something was going wrong. Patch struggled with the shaking steering wheel, trying to get it back under his control, but it was too far gone to obey him. Joe turned in his seat, and saw the billowing cloud of thick smoke, the fingers of flame curling up from the back of the car. "Patch!" he cried.

Santa's sleigh was close behind the Patchmobile now, gaining fast.

"Do something!" Cornelia cried.

Santa's brow wrinkled with desperate concern as he tried to think of some way to save them.... "The Super-Dooper-Looper!" he cried suddenly. "Come on, Donner. You can do it, boy!"

The two lead reindeer ducked their heads obediently and started sharply downward, pulling the sleigh after them as they swept below and beneath the smoking Patchmobile, gathering momentum to begin their tremendous loop. The reindeer and sleigh began to climb again, rising upward more and more steeply.

Patch jammed on the brakes in a frantic effort to avoid a collision. At the same moment, the candy canes exploded, blowing the Patchmobile apart. Its two terrified occupants were flung straight up into the sky. They reached the top of their own arc just as the looping sleigh reached its zenith, and then they began to plummet down again through the air.

The flying reindeer and sleigh swooped down like a roller coaster through the final arc of its loop, reaching bottom at the last, the only, possible second for a midair rendezvous. The plummeting boy and elf crashed down into the back of the sleigh, a human cargo more precious to Santa Claus and Cornelia than a hundred sacks of toys.

Santa laughed for the first time in far too long, "We did it!" he cried. "We did it!"

The sleigh and its rejoicing crew flew on toward the North Pole, and an even happier reunion.

The new day found B.Z. at his desk in his private office, gloating over the latest figures on his ill-gotten gains from candy canes.

Outside, far below him, five blue-and-white squad cars had surrounded the office building. There were police everywhere, rushing from all sides toward the building entrance.

At the sight of them, B.Z.'s eyes bulged with pure terror. He had no way of knowing, any more than Cornelia did, that the police had indeed believed her story.

"You'll never get me, coppers," he mumbled unintelligibly. B.Z. rushed to his office window, flung it open and leaped.

The crowd of policemen began to point and shout; their warnings turned into disbelief in midcry: instead of falling, their quarry was shooting straight up into the air like a rocket, propelled by a mega-overdose of magic candy canes.

B.Z. let out a howl of outrage that should have echoed around the world. "*Get me down! Get me out of here!*" he bellowed.

But, as they say, in space no one can hear you scream. B.Z. rolled on through the blackness, kicking and screaming gracelessly into that good night.

And at the North Pole, its inhabitants gathered in the Great Hall for a noisy, joyful celebration.

Patch took a deep breath, straightening his shoulders. "Santa Claus," he said, and including all his fellow elves in his glance, "starting right now I'm going to start a course of elf-improvement and make you proud."

Joe, feeling suddenly lost and more like an orphan than ever, began to wander away from the crowd.

But Santa followed Joe into a quiet corner.

"Joe," Santa asked quietly, "isn't there *anything* you want?"

Suddenly the words came bursting out in a flood. "I want to stay with you. I want to be your kid."

Cornelia's mouth quivered, then firmed with resolution as she asked, "Can I stay too?"

Santa turned to Anya, seeing the sudden shining eagerness in her own eyes. How did that old song go, he thought, *A boy for me and a girl for you...?*

Hastily he considered the sudden logistics and added requirements of having two children at the North Pole.

"Well...," he murmured, stroking his beard. He glanced at the two waiting children again, and nodded decisively. "Dooley—" he called, summoning his trusted advisor.

Dooley grinned and said with mock exasperation, "As if I don't have enough to do, now I'm going to have to be a schoolteacher!"

Joe and Cornelia looked at each other in sudden dismay. *"School??"* they chorused, their faces falling. Santa Claus began to laugh, his merry *ho-ho-ho* ringing out across the hall. He was happier than he had ever been in his life...and that was a considerable amount of time.

In the perfect stillness of the polar night, the lights began to wink out one by one, the elves' village slowly melting into the greater darkness. And, gentle reader, if you believe in Santa Claus in your own secret heart—in the spirit of loving generosity, in the true and sometimes almost-forgotten meaning of Christmas—you may glimpse those twinkling lights in the darkness when you dream tonight.